Pictures

presents

A Kid in King Arthur's Court

A Novel by ANNE MAZER

Based on the Motion Picture from WALT DISNEY PICTURES

In Association with TRIMARK PICTURES and TAPESTRY FILMS

Executive Producer MARK AMIN

Co-Producers ANDREW HERSH   JONATHON KOMACK MARTIN

Based on the Screenplay Written by MICHAEL PART & ROBERT L. LEVY

Produced by ROBERT L. LEVY PETER ABRAMS J. P. GUERIN

Directed by MICHAEL GOTTLIEB

Disney
PRESS

New York

First Disney Press Paperback Edition

© 1995 by Buena Vista Pictures Distribution, Inc.

The stories, characters, and/or incidents in this publication are entirely fictional.

Printed in the United States of America.

1   3   5   7   9   10   8   6   4   2

This book is set in 12-point Esprit Book.

Designed by Lara S. Demberg.

Library of Congress Catalog Card Number: 95-70037
ISBN: 0-7868-4069-2 (paperback)

A Kid in King Arthur's Court

CONTENTS

I
WANTED: A KNIGHT

King Arthur's sanctuary had been deserted for many years. Dust was thick on the royal suit of armor and on the King's sword, Excalibur, lying useless in its wooden rack. The Well of Destiny, with its dark, brooding waters, lay still and untroubled.

Suddenly, the water in the well rippled. The image of the great magician Merlin appeared. While he threw colored powders, bugs, lizards, and snakes into a golden chalice, he intoned magical words:

"Camelot is shrouded in evil and darkness. It grips the heart of King Arthur Pendragon. I call out from the netherworld, across all time, to seek a strong knight who can wield the sword Excalibur. A brave warrior who will protect the kingdom from creatures that never see the light . . . O great Cup of Life—bring me that knight!"

The image faded. Once more the Well of Destiny lay still and untroubled.

* * *

"I can't do it, Dad," Calvin Fuller said. His shoulders slumped in dejection. "There's no way I can play today."

"Of course you can, Calvin," his father reassured him.

"You're scared!" taunted his younger sister, Maya.

"No, I'm not!"

Calvin and his family were walking toward the baseball diamond where his Little League team, the Knights, were about to play a big game. He was worried: the other team's pitcher, Ricky Baker, had a ferocious reputation. And he always struck Calvin out.

"You're not a bad player, Cal," his father continued. "Face your fears. Walk through them."

"Walking isn't my problem. It's swinging the bat."

"You don't want to let your team down, do you, Son?" His father patted him on the back. "Have a little faith in yourself."

"Yeah, right, Dad," Cal said glumly. "Have you seen this guy's fastball?"

A few minutes later, Calvin sat on the far end of the team bench, trying to look inconspicuous and wishing hopelessly that he wouldn't be called up to bat. Just the *name* Ricky Baker gave him the chills.

"You're up, Fuller!" shouted the coach.

There was no avoiding it now. Calvin stood and walked slowly toward the plate.

"Ventilate him, Calvin!" yelled one of his teammates.

"Try swinging this time, Fuller." That was Howell, the perfect athlete, a Greek god among the geeks like Calvin.

"It's only a game, Son," his father called from the stands. "Just give it your best shot."

"Good luck, honey, we're all rooting for you," his mother said.

"If you get killed, I get your room!" Maya said as she leaned on the fence.

"If I die, you get to take out the garbage!" Calvin shot back.

Calvin walked to the batter's box, got his bat, and stepped up to the plate. There he stood, looking straight at Ricky Baker.

Ricky Baker grinned maniacally and slapped the ball into his glove. "You're dead meat, Fuller."

The coach walked over. "Look," he said to Calvin. "Just remember what I told you. Three things. Lean in. Cover the plate. Pick a point in the outfield . . . and let her rip."

"Actually that's four," Calvin said.

The coach rolled his eyes. "Just try and hit the ball, Fuller, will ya?"

"Three things . . ." Calvin muttered to himself. Could he do it?

The ball whizzed by him and thudded into the catcher's mitt.

"Strike one!" the umpire called.

He took a deep breath and positioned himself again at the plate. He didn't want to let his teammates down! That would be the worst.

"OhGodohGodohGodohGodohGod . . ." he whispered, raising his bat.

THUNK! The ball had hit the catcher's mitt.

"Strike two!" the umpire called.

"*Hasta la vista*, Fuller," Ricky Baker sneered.

Calvin snapped his gaze back to the coach. The

team . . . his friends . . . Dad, Mom, Maya. . . . He couldn't disappoint them. . . .

Ricky Baker wound up once more. His arm went back, his leg went up. Then he threw . . . THOK! Calvin hadn't even swung once.

"Steeee-rike three!" the umpire yelled. "You're owwwwwt!"

Calvin walked back to the bench with lowered head. His teammates turned away as he passed.

"Siddown," the coach ordered him. "Howell, you're up!"

Howell, the perfect athlete, grabbed Calvin by the shoulder. "Fuller," he commanded. "Get me my bat."

"Yes, your highness," Calvin muttered.

As he pulled out the biggest bat in the rack, the earth began to rumble and shake.

"Earthquake!" yelled the coach. "Everyone out of the dugout!"

The boys scattered. Calvin ran, heading for his family, when he suddenly remembered his backpack. All of his most prized possessions were inside it. His portable CD player, his Rollerblades, his Swiss Army knife . . . everything he loved. He turned, dashed back to the dugout, and snatched it from under the bench. The earth opened up beneath him.

The next thing he knew, he was falling, tumbling. All around him it was dark. "Coach! Help!" he cried. He fell and fell and fell . . . "Mom! Dad! HELP!" No one answered.

Down he went, deep into the earth. In the distance, a tiny light flickered. As he fell toward it, the light grew larger, stronger, brighter. . . .

II

ENCOUNTER WITH A KING

In another time, and another place, long before anyone had heard of baseball games, personal stereos, or strikeouts, a Black Knight gripped a money box under his arm, and galloped quickly away from the King's carriage.

"Stop him! He's stolen the royal money box!" King Arthur shouted as he leaned out of his carriage. His hands shook. This was no longer the vigorous, masterful king of legend: His face looked weary and old; his royal robes were in disarray; his crown was tarnished.

At his command, a squad of royal guards took off in pursuit of the Black Knight.

Suddenly, a vortex of light opened above the King. Out tumbled a stunned-looking Calvin, still wearing his Knights baseball uniform. He fell from the sky, landing squarely on the Black Knight.

Thief, money box, and boy fell to the ground. Calvin found himself face-to-face with the Black Knight. It was a fearsome sight—even for one who had recently faced Ricky Baker. As Calvin screamed in terror, the Black Knight looked around. The guards were closing in on him. With a regretful glance at the money box, the Black Knight leaped on his horse and galloped away.

Calvin knelt down and opened the box. It was full of gold! He stared at the shining pieces in amazement. Knights in armor, gold pieces, galloping steeds . . . what kind of place had he come to? Calvin didn't have any time to wonder. Guards were rushing toward him. And from the looks on their faces, he could tell they thought *he* was the thief! He jumped to his feet, abandoning the money box, and ran for his life into the forest.

*   *   *

Ratan, the High Chamberlain, leader of the King's Guard, had a body that mirrored his soul: twisted, scarred, and deformed. Lank dark hair hung over his ugly face. He retrieved the stolen money box and replaced it in the King's carriage. Then he looked up. Lord Belasco reined in his horse. He was elegant, dangerous, and perfectly groomed, with a distinctive lightning bolt of white through his dark hair. The two men locked eyes. A silent current of conspiracy flowed between them.

King Arthur appeared in the carriage window. "Find the brave man who foiled the Black Knight," he commanded in a wavering voice. "I want to thank him personally."

None of the guards moved until Lord Belasco gave a slight nod. Then Ratan and the others galloped off in search of Calvin.

"Thank you, Lord Belasco," said Arthur, smiling anxiously.

"My pleasure, Your Majesty." Belasco bowed slightly. He pretended to be the obedient servant and the great King Arthur was putty in his hands.

* * *

Calvin, panting, stopped dead in his tracks. Towering before him, rising above the trees, was a magnificent castle unlike any of the wonders of twentieth-century California. He wanted to stop and stare at it for a long time, but the sounds of horsemen in pursuit were growing louder.

As he sprinted down a hill and into a village, people gawked at his blue baseball jersey and baseball cap. They too wore costumes Calvin had never seen before. But there was no time to waste in wondering about this strange place. Ratan and the guards were coming closer. Calvin ran down an alley, dove through a window, and found himself in a dark, crowded store. He quickly ducked behind some nearby barrels.

Only moments later, Ratan and his guards entered the store. The owner held out empty hands. "There is nothing left to steal in all of Camelot!"

"Camelot . . ." Calvin silently repeated to himself in awe. Knights and ladies! Arthur and the Round Table! He was in the Middle Ages!

Ratan grabbed the owner by the collar. "The King does not steal," he snarled. "He merely takes his fair share."

"In other words, everything," muttered the owner.

Ratan shoved him aside. "I have no more time for this. We are looking for a boy."

A woman had entered the shop during their

exchange. Now she pulled the shopkeeper to one side and said in a hushed voice, "Do not fight him, shopkeeper! The King is no longer a man of the people! He surrounds himself with evil men!"

"You speak treason, woman!" Ratan pushed her against Calvin's hiding place. The barrels rolled aside.

"Ah, the little mouse!" Ratan cried.

Calvin dodged under his legs, charged out the door, and ran straight into the arms of the head guard.

"Don't kill me! I didn't mean to fall on the Black Knight!" he babbled frantically. "I don't know what happened! I don't belong here! Look—I don't even have a sword!"

The head guard clapped his hand over Calvin's mouth.

"Take him to Camelot," ordered Ratan. "The King awaits his presence."

"The King?" came Calvin's muffled voice.

"Yes," sneered Ratan. "'Tis his royal command."

As the guards seized Calvin's arms and marched him away toward the castle, he repeated incredulously, "The King wants to meet *me*?"

*   *   *

Lord Belasco stormed up to Ratan. "Did you find him?" he demanded.

"Of course," Ratan said.

"Well, bring him to me," Lord Belasco ordered coldly.

"He—he was taken to the Great Hall. The King—"

Lord Belasco cut him off. "You take orders from me—not that old fool!"

He grabbed Ratan by the neck and slammed him against the stone wall. "I finally have Arthur where I want him—the Black Knight is working his magic perfectly—and I will not have interlopers like this boy spoiling things. You are my High Chamberlain. Take charge!" He stalked off before his henchman could answer.

*   *   *

In the Great Hall, King Arthur sat at a huge rectangular table with his two daughters, Katey and Sarah. It was dinner time. Musicians played; jugglers juggled; attendants served great platters of meat and fowl and scurried about clearing away the picked-over bones.

The great oak door swung open. A guard shoved Calvin forward. He stumbled into the room, the door slamming behind him with a resounding bang.

"Ah." Arthur squinted nearsightedly in Calvin's direction. "The brave man who frightened off the Black Knight. Bring him close."

"Not a man, Father," his older daughter, Sarah, corrected him. She was a poised, attractive, and self-assured young woman of twenty. "Just a boy."

"He has a very pleasant face," said the younger daughter, Katey. She looked about fourteen, Calvin thought, just his age. Her dark hair fell loosely to her shoulders, and two braids were pulled back from her face.

"Shhhh! Don't be ridiculous, sister," hissed Sarah. "He dresses like a fool."

Katey stared at Calvin. Their eyes met. Calvin felt his heart began to race.

"Dost thou know who *I* am, lad?" interrupted Arthur.

"Um—the King?" Calvin answered.

"Yes, that's right." Arthur paused dramatically. "*I* am King Arthur."

"Cool."

"Cool?" Arthur asked. He looked puzzled for a moment, but then his face cleared. "Ah!" He snapped his fingers. Two servants dropped a huge mangy fur over Calvin's shoulders. The weight of it pushed him to the floor. It didn't smell too good, either.

He peeked out from under a corner. "Is this thing dead?"

The door flew open and Lord Belasco strode in.

"Your Majesty!" He grabbed Calvin's arm roughly, hauling him to his feet. "This boy is obviously in league with the Black Knight."

"Who, me?" Calvin protested, aghast. "No, I'm not!"

"'Tis obvious," Belasco continued, "he is nothing more than a common spy."

"What?" Calvin cried. He turned to Arthur. "I don't know how I got here, Your Honor, but I'm not a spy!"

Arthur leaned over the table toward Calvin. "You have been challenged, boy. Step up and prove yourself worthy." Then he turned toward Belasco. "You will allow him an opportunity to choose his mode of combat."

Belasco nodded, and bowed with a flourish.

"Combat?" Calvin echoed. This was serious. He could die. "No, wait—let's talk about this for a minute. . . ."

When no one answered, he began to slap himself, first on one cheek, then on the other. "Wake up, Calvin. Wake up, buddy." He slapped harder. "WAKE UP!"

He stared around the Great Hall. It was still there. The King was still there. And the two Princesses were looking at him expectantly. "Oh, no!" he moaned. "It's not a dream!"

"Quite right," Belasco agreed. " 'Tis your worst nightmare." His voice became icy. "Choose."

"Right." Calvin pulled himself together. "Okay. Mode of combat, right?" He looked anxiously around the Great Hall as everyone awaited his answer. His eyes stopped for a moment on the sentry horns. Middle Ages communication. Cool. Without thinking, he fingered his headset. Suddenly his face lit up.

"Okay," he said. "You want a mode of combat? You got it. I choose—combat rock!"

He glanced quickly around the room. The lords and ladies watched him with puzzled expressions on their faces. Calvin walked over to the center of the room and pushed the two sentry horns wide apart. Then he took the headphones from his portable CD player and pulled the wires apart, putting one of the earphones in the left horn, and the other in the right.

The King and his daughters, the knights and nobles all looked puzzled. Calvin pulled a shiny compact disc from his backpack and flashed it so it caught the light. He put it in the player, cranked up the volume as loud as it could go, and said to Belasco, "Top this!" Then he pushed play.

Ladies screamed and men cowered as the hall

vibrated to the sounds of rock and roll music. Calvin pantomimed playing the guitar, then did a few dance steps back to his portable CD player. He looked around once more, then clicked it off. There was utter silence.

Slowly Arthur got to his feet. The knights and ladies broke into enthusiastic applause.

"'Tis a miracle!" Arthur said.

"Yes, sir," Calvin answered proudly. "In full-blown digital stereo."

"I have never heard such a clamor in all my days."

"That was no clamor, Your Highness. That was rock and roll!"

Arthur turned to Belasco. "Lord Belasco, what say you?"

Belasco couldn't speak. He glared at Calvin and stormed out of the Great Hall.

The King looked pleased. "Sit beside me, lad!"

As Calvin made his way over to the King, Sarah came close and whispered anxiously in his ear, "Be very careful, sir. You have made a powerful enemy today."

"Who, me?" Calvin asked, still giddy from his triumph.

"What do they call thee, boy?" asked Arthur. "And from whence do you hail?"

"Calvin Fuller, sir. From Reseda."

"Knights and ladies," boomed the King, in formal introduction. "I give you Calvin Fuller of Reseda."

*   *   *

Calvin stared at the plate of food that had just been put in front of him. "It, uh, looks real good." He didn't want to be rude, but he wasn't putting it in his mouth, either. "What *is* it?"

"A rare treat, fit for a king," said Arthur, taking a large bite from his own plate. "Braised boar's snout and haggis. Eat up, boy!"

"Uh—no, thanks." Calvin tried not to gag. "I think I'll stick with dessert."

Katey leaned over toward Calvin. "I heard of what transpired between you and the Black Knight. You are incredibly brave."

"I'm glad you think so." Calvin's heart was thumping madly again. "Who is this Black Knight guy, anyway?"

"A scoundrel!" said Katey fiercely. "His mission is to bring down my father's kingdom. I wish he were dead." She nodded at Calvin's untouched plate of food. "Eat. It loses its bouquet when it is taken cold."

Calvin raised a forkful to his mouth, then abruptly brought it down again. The smell alone was enough to kill a person! "Say, where's Merlin?" he asked. "When does he show up?"

"Sadly, Merlin is no more," said Katey. "He passed away many years ago." She paused. "Eat. You'll feel much better."

Calvin forced himself to put a bit of the vile stuff in his mouth. But then he quickly spat it out on the floor. A pack of Irish wolfhounds rushed up to devour it. Lucky for him, no one had noticed. He wouldn't want to insult the King.

"Uhhhh, excuse me, Your Highness." Something was puzzling Calvin. "I don't mean to butt in here, but isn't there something missing? Like the Round Table?"

"Round Table?" Arthur frowned. "I know not of what you speak, lad."

"Come on! You invented it! It's where you and your knights have your meetings." Calvin took a breath and continued. "It's round, so you gotta look everybody in the eye. No favorites. Everybody's equal."

Arthur stared at him. "Everybody's equal . . . fascinating idea."

Sarah approached her father. "If I may be so bold, Father, may I suggest for our honored visitor from Reseda, a fortnight of training with Master Kane?"

Training for what, Calvin thought nervously. He was bad enough at baseball. "Uh, I don't like the sound of this—" he began.

"Splendid idea, Daughter," Arthur said. He turned to Calvin. "Tomorrow my Master at Arms will instruct you in the ways of the Knights of Camelot. Perhaps we may learn from each other."

III
THE KING'S SANCTUARY

 "Welcome to Camelot, sir." The lady-in-waiting turned down Calvin's bed and left. Calvin stared. He couldn't believe this room. It was a lot better than any motel room his parents had ever checked them into on vacations. The bed was magnificent. His walls were covered with ancient druid runes. There was an elaborate armoire against one wall. But where was the bathroom?

He crossed to the armoire and opened the door. It was full of old clothes, boots, and nightshirts that smelled musty. "Nope. Must be down the hall," he said to himself.

He left his room. As he hurried around a corner, he smacked right into Lord Belasco.

"Lord Elastic!" he cried, jumping back.

"Be-las-co," said Lord Belasco, pronouncing each syllable with icy precision as he advanced slowly toward Calvin.

Calvin backed away. He wished a door would open in the wall and save him. Even a hole in the floor would do. Instead he backed into solid stone. There was nowhere to run! Belasco had him cornered!

"Shhhh . . . listen," Belasco hissed.

"What?" Calvin said. "I don't hear anything."

"Exactly." Lord Belasco pushed his face directly into Calvin's. "I can choke the life from you right here—and no one would even hear you scream."

Calvin couldn't believe this Belasco guy. He made Ricky Baker look like a wimp. "Hold on to that thought," he said, darting out from Belasco's grasp. He ran back to his room and slammed the door behind him. Safe! But he still hadn't found a bathroom.

As he looked around, something white and gleaming under the bed caught his eye. He pulled it out. A chamber pot. He sighed. "You gotta be kidding . . ."

*   *   *

Before he went to sleep, Calvin stripped down to his boxer shorts and practiced his karate moves. He wasn't an expert, but he *had* studied for a few years. He did a few kicks and punches, then some jump kicks, and a couple of *katas*. Then he took out his nunchaku, twirling them expertly in the air.

The door opened a crack. Someone was watching him. Was it Belasco? He yanked it open. A very embarrassed Katey tumbled in.

"Oh! Excuse me, good sir! Pardon my intrusion!" she apologized. "My father asked that I make sure thou art comfortable in your new quarters."

"You want me comfortable?" Calvin asked. "How about getting me a road map out of the Middle Ages? If I don't get home, I'm grounded."

Katey's eyes wandered to his boxer shorts. "You Resedians wear very strange garments."

It was his turn to be embarrassed. "Would you mind, uh . . ."

Katey smiled and turned away. Calvin snatched his baseball pants and pulled them on. Something she had said didn't fit. She was a *princess*. "Wait a minute," he said. "Your *father* sent you here?"

"I cannot lie to thee." Katey looked down. "My

father knows nothing of my nocturnal transgressions, sir."

"Do me a favor?" he asked. "Call me Calvin."

She nodded shyly. "That dance. What was it?"

"Dance?" He had done a few dance steps in the Great Hall to the rock and roll music. He couldn't believe she remembered.

"You know…" She began to imitate his karate moves.

"Oh, that!" He grinned. "That's not a dance. It's karate. There was this kid who beat me up every day and stole my lunch money. So my dad signed me up for karate school." He sighed, thinking of his family. "I really miss them. My sister, too. I never thought I'd say that." He looked at Katey. "You have no idea what I'm talking about, do you?"

Katey shook her head. "I fear I know nothing of karate or lunch money. But I *do* know what it is like to miss one's parents. My father has never been the same since Mother died. I miss my mother deeply; but I miss my father even more."

At her words, Calvin felt an even more intense wave of longing for his parents and sister. He turned to Katey and blurted, "Can you help me, Katey? I really need to go home."

"I truly cannot," Katey said gently. "But perhaps there is someone who can."

"Really? Who?"

"Merlin."

"Merlin?" Calvin frowned. "But you said he was dead."

Katey smiled. "Not quite."

She went to the wall and felt along it, stopping at one of the runes. She pushed, and listened for the click. A panel in the wall slowly opened.

Calvin gaped as Katey took a candle and disappeared into the cavernous darkness of the passage.

Then she stuck her head out. "Come!"

Calvin grabbed his backpack and followed her.

Katey stopped in the middle of the passage as her candle flickered dimly. Ahead, all was darkness, and she had no idea where to find the other rune she needed. "Alas, this candle sheds not enough light," she said, shivering.

"You think *that's* a candle?" Calvin pulled out a mini-flashlight from his backpack and clicked it on. The passage brightened dramatically. "*This* is a candle."

"It's incredible," Katy breathed. One by one she checked the runes on the wall until she found the right one. There was a click, and another section of the wall creaked open.

"These were once Merlin's quarters," Katey said.

"Now they are my father's private sanctuary."

Calvin was hardly listening. His eyes were riveted on a magnificent sword. The King's sword. Excalibur. The sword of legends.

He pointed at it, stammering in his excitement. "Wow! Is that . . . no! It can't be . . ."

"Oh, that?" Katey shrugged. "That is just Father's old sword."

"Old sword? That's Excalibur!" Calvin breathed.

"My, thou *dost* know a lot." She looked at him admiringly.

Reverently, Calvin approached the sword. It was covered with a thick layer of grime. He leaned over and blew on it. A cloud of dust filled the air.

Calvin turned to Katey. "No one has touched it in years." He shook his head in disbelief.

" 'Tis true," Katey's voice was sad. She beckoned to him again and led him to a pool of water circled by a stone wall.

Calvin stared. "Wow, you even have a hot tub. . . . "

" 'Tis the Well of Destiny," Katey explained.

The water swirled and then became glassy. A great, ancient book appeared in its depths.

"This is all that is left of Merlin," said Katey. "His Book of Spells. If there is a way home—the answer will be in there."

Calvin rolled up his sleeve and knelt down in front of the pool. Just as he eased his hand into the water for the book, he heard footsteps approaching in the passage outside. Katey yanked him away. "Quick! Someone comes! We must fly!"

They hid behind heavy curtains, then slipped back into the passage. The door slammed behind them. They ran through the dark corridor until they came to Katey's door.

"Here is where we must part." She studied him tenderly. "There is something special about you, Calvin of Reseda. Perhaps your arrival is no accident."

She pressed a rune on the door and it slid open.

Calvin watched her step into her room. She was so pretty. The door was about to close when he realized he didn't know where he was or how to get to his room. "Hey—how do *I* get back?"

"Follow the wall. It stops at your quarters." Katey gazed at him one last time. "Good night, sir."

The wall closed firmly. Calvin leaned against it, thinking dreamily of Katey. It was really too bad she didn't live in the twentieth century. With a sigh, he turned in the direction of his room. Then he stopped and looked back toward the King's sanctuary. . . .

*   *   *

Calvin stood hidden in the curtains, watching Arthur in his sanctuary. The once-great King approached his ancient sword, Excalibur, with deep respect, and tried to lift it from its casing. But the sword did not budge.

"What sorcery is this, Merlin," Arthur cried out in despair, "that I can no longer brandish the sword Excalibur? Are you reaching out from your grave to stop me?"

No answer came to the King's cry.

"Of course you are not," he said sadly. "Excalibur . . . I thought we would reign forever." Arthur buried his face in his hands. "I was wrong. Camelot rots . . . and I play at being king."

For a moment he was silent. Behind the curtains Calvin hardly dared breathe.

"I want Camelot great again," King Arthur said quietly. "But I fear I am too weak to bring her back." With one last grieving look at Excalibur, he left the sanctuary.

As soon as he was sure it was safe, Calvin tiptoed over to the sword and touched its hilt gently. Then once again he went to the Well of Destiny and this time thrust his hand fully into the icy water. The Book of Spells wavered beneath his touch, tantalizingly almost-real. Merlin, Calvin thought, are you dead or are you alive?

The water clouded. Merlin's face appeared in the depths of the well. His voice boomed out powerfully. "My powers fail me! I cast a spell for a knight who can wield Excalibur—and all I get is a boy!"

"Ohhh," said Calvin. "You wanted Howell. *Everybody* wants him on their team." Suddenly he realized who he was talking to. "You're Merlin! *You* brought me here!"

"Unfortunately," the magician said dryly.

"Cool!" A cloak dropped on him. Calvin crawled out from under it. "Where'd *that* come from?"

"I thought you requested it," Merlin said. "Matters not. Now that we have you—what are we going to do with you?"

"I'm just trying to get home, Your Honor. I mean, your wizardry—your wetness," Calvin stammered. "The Princess said . . ."

"SILENCE!" roared Merlin. He gazed sternly at Calvin. "Because I brought you here, I can grant you safe passage home. But first you must prove yourself."

"Okay. What do you want me to do?" Calvin said. He was ready to do anything. As long as it got him out of the Middle Ages. Now. "Go on a quest?

Fight a dragon? Rescue some damsels . . ."

Merlin held up his hand to silence him. "Deliver Camelot."

Calvin was too stunned to utter even a word of protest.

"Arthur was once a courageous king," Merlin continued. "But sadly, no more. He believes not in himself. And so his people are set adrift on a sea of torment."

"Whoa. I can totally relate," Calvin burst out. "Whenever I go against this one pitcher—Ricky Baker. Maybe you've heard of him? Anyway, every time I bat against him I go Absolute Zero. I don't know if it's the way he looks at me, or maybe it's just the way he looks—"

"ENOUGH!" Merlin paused. His eyes bulged beneath the water. "Help Arthur find his way back—and I'll help you find yours."

His reflection rippled and vanished, leaving a still pool of water in the Well of Destiny.

IV
KNIGHT IN TRAINING

 Calvin watched a knight on a barrel horse being pulled toward a straw-man dummy on wooden gimbals. If the knight missed, the thing was rigged so he would get a hearty club on the back. Bet they learn fast around here, Calvin thought.

The knight swung his battle axe with expert precision and neatly beheaded the dummy.

Kane, the Master of Arms, took the battle axe from the knight. "Nicely done," he said.

"Thank you." The knight pulled off the helmet and long dark hair tumbled to her shoulders. It was Katey!

"Would you care to show us how it is done in Reseda?" she asked, in response to Calvin's astonished stare.

"Actually, I was hoping for a desk job," he said. His legs felt a little weak.

"As of today thou art a knight in training." Master Kane indicated the barrel horse.

Calvin stepped backward. "Thanks, but I won't be here that long. . . ."

"Don't tell me a brave lad such as thee who faced the Black Knight in all his fury is frightened of a straw dummy," began Kane.

"No way," Calvin said quickly. He didn't want Katey to see he was scared. "I was just testing you."

Katey took the battle axe from Master Kane and held it out to Calvin. "Proceed," she said sweetly.

Calvin staggered under the weight of the axe. "Wow, these things are heavier than they look on TV."

"Tee-vee?" asked Katey. "One of your knights of Reseda?"

"Something like that," Calvin said.

Katey took a visored helmet and fitted it on his head.

"Good fit," Kane said. "Canst thou see?"

"Perfectly." Calvin said. He turned and walked straight into a wall.

Next came the barrel horse. He got stuck with one leg over and the other down. As he struggled to free himself, he clanked noisily to the floor.

Katey rushed over. "Are you all right?" she cried.

"Yeah," said Calvin, trying to salvage his dignity. With a little help from Master Kane, he got back on the horse.

*   *   *

As knights sparred and fought with axes and broadswords, Kane coached Calvin. "Remember what I told thee. Three things. Lean in. Cover thy steed. Fix a point on thy opponent's person. And have at him."

"That's four things," Calvin pointed out.

Master Kane looked puzzled. "What?"

"Never mind." Calvin smiled and nodded to Katey. "Hit it."

As two squires pulled the barrel horse toward a new straw-man dummy, Calvin swung his axe—and missed. The dummy thunked him on the back. The axe flew from his hands and twirled out the window. There was a faint splash as it fell into the moat.

Next came archery practice. Master Kane instructed the other knights; Katey shot bull's-eyes; and Calvin struggled with his bow and arrow.

"I thought all knights spent their time rescuing damsels and fighting dragons," he said, gesturing toward the other knights. "What are they all doing here?"

"They are training hard for the big tournament," Katey answered. "You see, the prize is quite appealing to all men of royal blood."

"Oh, really? What is it?"

"My sister. And Camelot."

Calvin was shocked. "What about her? Doesn't she have a choice?"

"She has refused all suitors," Katey said. "So on her twenty-first birthday the tournament will decide for her."

"Bummer."

"I think I agree."

She pulled back her arrow and shot another bull's-eye. "Now you try."

Calvin pulled the arrow back just as Katey had done. Then he let go. The arrow flew past the target and over the castle wall. A faint splash was heard as the arrow, too, landed in the moat.

V
LEARNING TO SKATE

 The flame fired white-hot as the blacksmith laid a raw sword into it and then drew it out and set it on an anvil. He paused for a moment to wipe the sweat from his brow.

"Hey, how's it going?" Calvin asked as he walked in with his backpack on.

"Ah, good sir. My shop is at your disposal."

"Really? Thanks." Calvin was a little nervous. He was about to ask a really big favor. "I hear you can make anything."

"Indeed, I have that reputation."

Calvin pulled a pair of Rollerblades from his backpack.

"By the circle builders themselves!" The blacksmith's eyes widened in wonder.

"I need another pair of these," Calvin told him. "I need them pretty fast. Like yesterday."

* * *

In the morning, Calvin was awakened by the sound of his window opening. He jumped up in alarm. "Who's there?"

"I trust you slept well," said Katey sweetly.

He hauled the covers up over his body. "We all did. Me and the forest of crawling things in my bed."

"Come," she said, turning away while he pulled on his clothes. "Breakfast is served in the Great Hall. We must hurry or we'll be late."

Calvin reached under his bed. "Wait a second. I have something to show you." He pulled out two pairs of Rollerblades—his and the pair made from steel, leather, and rope.

* * *

Calvin and Katey Rollerbladed hand-in-hand through the corridors of King Arthur's castle. They turned, jumped steps, and whizzed past various astonished guards.

"But I don't understand," Katey said as they rolled through the halls. "If it's bad—it's good?"

Calvin had been trying to teach Katey a few of his favorite expressions. "Yeah. If it's cool, it's hot."

"Oh, I fear I will never understand your Valley-speak," Katey sighed.

* * *

While Katey and Calvin were Rollerblading, Katey's older sister, Sarah, was in the garden, collecting flowers. Lord Belasco strolled toward her and pulled a long-stemmed rose from her basket.

He held it up. "Thou art the loveliest flower in the garden, Princess," he said smoothly.

Sarah plucked the flower from his fingers. "There is one major difference between the garden flowers and myself, Lord Belasco." She twirled the rose delicately. "The rose will prick you—but I will do far worse."

Lord Belasco studied her for a moment. This was more resistance than he had expected. "My Princess, you cut me to the quick," he said. "I want only what is best for my King and kingdom. We could make it great again."

Sarah raised one eyebrow inquiringly. "We?"

"Of course. The two of us. In wedded bliss." He waited for her answer confidently. He was not the king, but he *was* the most powerful man in Camelot.

Sarah stared at him coldly. "I will marry the man who wins the tournament. Enter it. *If* you have the brass. Good day, sir."

*   *   *

King Arthur sat at the newly constructed Round Table. "Nobody could call me a fussy man," he said plaintively, "but I do like a little bit of butter on me bread."

Just then Lord Belasco burst into the Great Hall.

The king put down his knife. "What is it you wish to speak to mc about, Lord Belasco?"

"Decisions, Your Excellency," Lord Belasco said crisply.

"Oh? Ah . . ." said Arthur. He sighed. Decisions were among his least favorite things.

"It is time you made some."

"Yes, of course. Of course," Arthur agreed, with another sigh. "What did you have in mind?"

"I have been loyal to you for many years. I only ask for one thing in return. Sarah's hand in marriage."

King Arthur's head jerked up. This was no annoying little decision of state. This was his daughter they were talking about. "Thou knowest the laws of Camelot," he said sternly, sounding almost like his old self. "The tournament shall decide for her."

"The fate of Camelot should not be left to the folly of a tournament," Belasco urged. "Should it, Your Majesty?" He fixed his most intimidating stare on the King.

Arthur picked up his bread with slow fingers. "I shall speak to my daughter on your behalf."

Lord Belasco bowed deeply. "Thank you, Your Majesty."

As he turned to leave, the door of the Great Hall flew open.

"All right, the Round Table!" Calvin cried joyously to King Arthur as he and Katey skated into the Great Hall together. "The history books are going to love you!"

Lord Belasco glared furiously at this impertinent intruder. The boy was always underfoot! Well, he wouldn't be around much longer. He and Ratan would take care of that. He stepped to the side and bumped hard into Calvin, pushing him off balance, almost knocking him to the ground.

Katey scowled at him. "Not staying for breakfast, Lord Belasco?" she said sarcastically.

"I do not wish to eat with children!" He stalked out of the Great Hall.

VI
A DUEL AND A MEAL

Carrying fighting staffs, Calvin and Master Kane headed toward the main gate of the castle.

"So where's *your* castle, Master Kane?" Calvin asked.

"Oh, I have no land of my own," shrugged the weapons master. Kane was handsome, strong, and good—but not rich or noble.

"Does that mean you can't enter the tournament?"

"Alas, the tournament is reserved for far better men than I."

"No way!" Calvin leaped to his teacher's defense. "You're the best!"

"If thou art trying to get on my good side, thou has succeeded with royal colors," grinned Kane. "Ah! Here is your opponent."

Calvin looked up. "You gotta be kidding." Katey was waiting for them on a stone bridge over the moat! "I can't fight the Princess."

"You are right about that, sir." Katey took the staff from Master Kane and slyly poked Calvin. "I wonder . . . do the knights of Reseda swim?"

Calvin readied his staff and they began to fight, attacking and blocking, according to the moves Master Kane had taught them.

"Thou hast much to learn before supper," Katey teased him as they fought. "I hear the kitchen is serving poached goat's tail in a brown grub sauce."

As Calvin's face twisted in revulsion, she continued, "Or perhaps we could hunt yon goose?"

He glanced hopefully up toward the sky, and at once Katey whacked him behind the knees, shoved her staff into his stomach, and toppled him over the wall into the stream.

Calvin emerged with a lily pad on his head and a sheepish expression on his face. "I can't believe I fell for the oldest trick in the book." He sighed. "Then again, since I'm here, maybe it's the *newest* trick in the book."

Master Kane shook his head. "Old or new, 'tis lesson number one. Never take your eyes off your opponent."

*   *   *

Princess Sarah entered the Great Hall, where her father sat on his throne. "You sent for me, Father?"

"I did? Oh yes, of course I did." He waved two guards away. "Out . . . out!"

He motioned his daughter closer. "I believe I know what is best for our kingdom . . ." he began, clearing his throat pompously. "A game to decide the fate of Camelot." He frowned. "I fear the tournament is an antiquated notion."

"You are dancing, Father," Sarah said coolly. "Get to the point."

Arthur gazed at her for a moment. This was his stubborn child. It was hard for him to say this, but say it he would. He summoned up memories of his old stern self. "I have decided . . ." he hesitated, then hurried on, ". . . that thou shalt marry Lord Belasco."

"No!" Sarah cried, recoiling. Her hands clenched into fists. "If I cannot marry for love, then the law of the land shall prevail. I shall let the tournament decide." She ran from the room without waiting for him to dismiss her.

"Oh, thou art as stubborn as thy mother," Arthur said softly and admiringly, shaking his head.

*　　*　　*

Back at Master Kane's practice yard, Calvin mounted the barrel horse, this time without falling. He was definitely improving. He took the broadsword confidently from Master Kane's hand.

"Guard it with your life," Master Kane warned him. "Unless you know how to swim."

Calvin nodded and readied himself. Then he leaned into the charge. "Go for it!"

The weapons master nodded. Squires pulled the barrel horse with Calvin astride. And this time, he swung the broadsword with perfect coordination, beheading the straw dummy.

Master Kane and Katey applauded enthusiastically. For a moment Calvin was so pleased he didn't even notice Belasco and Ratan entering the practice room. Then he saw them. They didn't look as if they had come to cheer him on.

"To what do we owe this unexpected pleasure, Lord Belasco?" Master Kane said politely.

"Out of my way, teacher." Belasco shoved him rudely aside.

Calvin hopped down from the barrel horse. This guy could use some lessons in manners.

"Perhaps now that thou art through fighting with straw men," Lord Belasco sneered, "thou wouldst like to face a real man." He drew his rapier.

"Boy, you guys are really hung up on this dominant male monkey thing, aren't you?" Calvin said.

Master Kane stepped forward to try and reason with Lord Belasco.

"This doesn't concern you, teacher." Lord Belasco faced Calvin. "I think I shall take your answer as a yes," he snarled.

He whipped his sword around and moved in on Calvin.

Calvin grabbed a staff to defend himself, but Lord Belasco's sword cut through it with one swoop. The evil lord smashed the hilt into Calvin's stomach and knocked him down.

As Calvin lay helpless on the ground, Lord Belasco towered over him, his sword raised, a grim smile on his face.

This is it, Calvin thought. He's got me now. But now all his hours of karate practice paid off. On pure reflex alone, he slammed his foot upward. Lord Belasco doubled over in pain, then dropped to his knees, his sword clattering to the ground.

Katey and the weapons master rushed to Calvin's side. "I could be wrong," Calvin said, his voice trembling just a little. "But I think I just qualified for a black belt."

"You had better hang yourself with it," Lord Belasco said as he rose shakily to his feet with Ratan's help. "Because when I come for thee, it will be far worse. Far, far worse . . ."

As the two men left the room, Calvin breathed a sigh of relief. "I think I'm the first person to get a contract taken out on him."

"You were very brave," said Katey.

"He tried to take my lunch money," Calvin explained.

Katey cast him a quick amused glance. "As a reward," she said, "thou hast earned a grand supper!"

Not another meal of boar and haggis! Calvin thought quickly. "On one condition," he said. "*I* do the cooking."

*   *   *

"The smell is divine!" Katey said. "What is it?"

"Ah-ah-ah. It's a surprise, Princess," Calvin answered.

Katey peeked out from under the blindfold Calvin had put over her eyes. "No!" she cried in horror as

Calvin sliced a tomato. "Those are poisonous love apples!"

"Trust me," Calvin said, grabbing a handful of seeds from a bag. "No peeking." He threw the seeds into a mortar with some water and ground them.

"Oh! Mustard seeds!" Katey looked sick. "We feed those to the pigs!"

Calvin laid down the his knife. "You're peeking, Princess." He pulled the blindfold back down over her eyes.

"It smells so wonderful," she admitted, "I cannot wait."

"Patience." He took cooked meat from the fireplace and brought it to the table. When everything was just right, he led Katey to her place at the table. "Okay, take off the blindfold," he said.

Katey clapped her hands. "It is beautiful," she breathed. "But *what is it?*"

"A meal fit for the Round Table." Calvin pulled up a chair and sat down opposite her. "Double cheeseburger with lettuce and tomatoes on a whole-wheat bun."

She took a big bite. "Mmm. Good . . ." She stopped. "I mean, bad!"

VII
CALVIN FOOLS KATEY

 The next day, Katey and Calvin rode out to meet Master Kane. From across the field, they could see him on his horse, lance lowered and ready, charging across the grass at a target propped on bales of hay. Bull's-eye! Kane reined in his steed and snapped open his helmet visor. He looked pleased.

Then as Calvin and Katey watched, they saw Sarah galloping out of the woods toward Master Kane. She reined in her horse next to him. They gazed at each other for a long moment, then shared a slow, romantic kiss.

"Avert thy eyes!" Katey ordered Calvin in an imperious tone of voice.

Sarah jerked her head up. When she saw her sister and Calvin at the other end of the field, she scowled in annoyance and rode swiftly away.

"You were not to see that," Katey said. She sounded as if she were scolding Calvin. "Swear your silence to me now, sir, or risk my wrath."

Calvin shrugged. "It's none of my business what your sister does."

"Swear it!" Katey insisted.

"Okay, okay, I swear it."

Master Kane rode up to them. "Art thou ready, lad?"

Calvin nodded, eyeing the lance nervously. Sparring with straw dummies or even Katey was one thing. This was something else entirely! "Can't we put this off till next Tuesday?" he suggested.

"No," said Master Kane. " 'Tis time to put a real lance in your hands."

The lance wobbled in Calvin's grip. Try as he might, he couldn't control it. It was heavier than he expected. How was he supposed to aim it from a galloping horse? And how was he ever going to keep from being thrown?

"Look," he said to Master Kane, "this is too

soon. I still get carsick on merry-go-rounds."

"Lean into the charge and the lance will do the work for thee," the weapons master advised.

"How about if *you* do the work for me?" Calvin suggested.

"Have you no confidence in yourself?" Katey asked.

Calvin took a deep breath. He wanted Katey to admire him, not to feel sorry for him or mock him. Then he had an inspiration. "Hey! Look at that two-headed dragon over there!"

As Katey and the weapons master whirled around to see, Calvin fished in his knapsack and whipped out a tube of Krazy Glue. Quickly, he rose from the saddle, squirted some on the seat, and sat back down, grinding the glue onto his pants.

"But I only see a tree," Master Kane said.

"Yeah, maybe I need to get my eyes checked," Calvin agreed.

Katey gave him a suspicious look. "Calvin, perhaps thou art not prepared?"

Calvin straightened his back. Who, him? He was prepared. As well as he'd ever be. "Let her rip, professor."

"He means yes," Katey translated to Master Kane.

Kane whacked the horse's flank, and they took

off. The target approached. Calvin readied his lance. The horse galloped up to the target. *Now, now, now!* Calvin thought, but he let go of the lance too late. It missed the target and drove straight into a tree.

He came unseated—and the seat came with him! He grabbed wildly at the lance, the saddle between his legs, as he bounced up and down like a bungee jumper. Then the lance snapped and he tumbled to the ground.

"Calvin!" cried Katey, running to him. She turned furiously to Kane. "Look what you've done! How could you?"

"But, Princess," Master Kane protested, "'twas you, who . . ."

"How *dare* you contradict me!" She gazed down at Calvin, who lay still with his eyes closed, then turned again on Kane. "This is *your* fault!"

While she scolded the weapons master, Calvin stole a quick peek from under half-closed eyes. He shut them swiftly again when Katey knelt by his side.

"Oh, sir, I am so sorry!" She touched his cheek gently. "Please speak to me!"

At her words, Calvin clumsily pulled her close and kissed her. For just a moment, it seemed like she kissed him back, but then she jerked away and jumped to her feet.

"You deceived me!" she said angrily, kicking him in the side. "You are impertinent!"

"Ouch!" Calvin cried. "Princess, wait!"

But she had already mounted her horse and was riding away.

Calvin stumbled slowly to his feet.

"Thou art a clever lad," said Master Kane, shaking his head.

Calvin nodded. "I think she likes me," he said, not taking his eyes off Katey's retreating back.

*   *   *

"I did not expect to see you so soon, sir." The blacksmith put down the sword he was forging. His muscles glistened in the heat of the shop. "Were not your bladerollers met with satisfaction?"

"They were killer, but this time I need something bigger." Calvin had another surprise for Katey—one that he hoped would make her forgive him. He went to the steel bin and picked out some scraps. "It's gotta be as light as a feather, but as hard as Lord Belasco's head. . . ."

"I know of no such metal!" the blacksmith protested.

"You will!" Calvin promised. He grabbed a piece

of tin armor and dumped the steel and the armor in front of the blacksmith. "Melt these together, stir, and then stand back."

A puzzled look crossed the blacksmith's face. "How can a boy know about smelting?"

"Metal shop," Calvin said. "Eighth grade."

*   *   *

"What are you eating, lad?" Arthur asked curiously, as he and Calvin sat on the floor of the Great Hall, playing with the dogs.

"Mad Dog Bubble Gum. Here." He handed the King a piece.

Arthur opened his mouth and swallowed it, wrapper and all.

"No!" Calvin cried. "You're not supposed to swallow it!"

"I'm not?"

Calvin took another piece of gum. This time, he unwrapped it first, then gave it to the King. "Just put it in your mouth and chew," he instructed.

"Chew . . ." said Arthur thoughtfully. He chewed . . . and chewed . . . and chewed. . . . "But if I cannot swallow, what is its purpose?" he burst out.

"There *is* no purpose," Calvin told him.

Arthur raised his eyebrows. "No purpose? Strange . . ."

Calvin blew a bubble and let it collapse on his face.

Arthur imitated him, chewing and blowing. Calvin nodded his approval.

"Why do they call it Mad Dog Bubble Gum?" The King asked. His mouth was covered with foam.

"I have no idea, Your Highness," Calvin said innocently.

A shadow fell across the room. The King started. His manner became troubled, almost cringing. "Ah. Lord Belasco. Have a seat."

"Get out, boy," Lord Belasco snarled.

Calvin looked questioningly at the King. He'd go only if Arthur said so.

"Affairs of the court, lad," the King said. "You understand."

"It's okay." Calvin rose. "I have a date."

"A date?" Arthur asked.

"I'll explain it to you later. . . ."

As soon as he was gone, Lord Belasco turned to King Arthur. "You spoke to your daughter?" he demanded icily.

Two guards rushed to the King's side to help him rise to his feet. "Yes, yes, of course . . ." he mumbled.

"And?"

"I cannot force her to marry thee," Arthur apologized weakly. "If she means that much to thee—there's always the tournament."

Lord Belasco's face registered fury. The tournament! How dare the King demand that he take part in a tournament? He didn't have to prove himself!

*　　*　　*

"She *will* be mine, or no one will have her!" Lord Belasco vowed furiously. He and Ratan were walking down one of the long castle corridors. He had never hated King Arthur quite so much. That pathetic old man! That doddering old fool! He would bend him to his will, sooner or later.

"Then you are planning to enter the tournament?" Ratan asked.

Lord Belasco grabbed him and shook him hard. "Of course not, you idiot! Why should I risk my life when there are other ways?"

VIII
A PICNIC

 Calvin paced nervously outside the castle, waiting for Katey. From time to time, he glanced at a mysterious object covered in cloth and leaning against the rampart wall.

"I came only because my music lessons were canceled." Katey had appeared, her head held high, her voice cool. "But you are still impertinent."

"I'll take that as a compliment," Calvin said.

"State your business," she directed, "then I shall be on my way."

"I have a surprise for you." He yanked the cloth from the mysterious object.

Katey stared in amazement, her anger already forgotten. "What is it?"

"A mountain bike," Calvin said proudly. The blacksmith had fashioned a frame from an alloy of iron and tin. The wooden wheels were held together with steel plates and rims. He had even linked forks and spoons to make the chain!

"What do you do with it?" she asked.

"In Reseda, we have a custom," Calvin told her. "It's called a picnic."

*   *   *

"This is better than Magic Mountain," Calvin sighed. He and Katey were having a picnic lunch in a lush meadow. The mountain bike lay in the grass nearby. Contented and happy, he looked over at Katey. She was staring moodily off into the distance.

"What's wrong?" he asked.

"Nothing . . ." Her voice was flat and toneless.

"Is it your father?"

She nodded.

"You know the night you took me to see Merlin's book?" Calvin confided in her. "I went back. I don't know if I'm going crazy or what, but—I saw Merlin in the well. . . ."

"He came to you?" Katey gasped.

"Yeah," Calvin said nervously. "He said he brought me here to save Camelot. Actually, he didn't bring *me* here—he meant to bring someone else . . ."

Katey put her hand gently on his. "He chose well."

"Thanks. I'm glad *someone* thinks so. It's my only ticket home." He glanced up and met her eye.

"What are the girls like—in Reseda?" Katey asked, blushing a little.

"Who knows?" Calvin said. Then he caught himself. "I mean, I don't know."

"Of course you do."

"They're nothing like you," he said warmly. He stood up and held out his hands to her. "I better get you home."

*   *   *

A crowd of hungry villagers surrounded a wagon overflowing with food and warm clothing, jostling one another to get closer. Their joyous cries filled the air. "It's truly a miracle! Food enough for all!"

On their way home from the picnic, Katey and Calvin paused to take the scene in. "Where did it all come from?" Katey asked.

In answer to her question, a quivering black arrow stabbed into the tree next to them. From a short distance, the Black Knight, astride a black stallion, was watching over the wagon to make sure all the goods were distributed fairly. Then he spurred his mount into the forest and disappeared.

Calvin's jaw dropped. Had he just seen what he thought he saw? "The Black Knight is one of the good guys?"

Katey frowned. "This cannot be true. . . ."

They looked at each other in confusion. Calvin wondered what it could mean. Was the Black Knight really their friend and not their enemy?

* * *

At dusk, as Calvin walked Katey into the castle, he asked, "Are you okay?"

"Confused," the Princess admitted.

He nodded. He understood. "About the Black Knight?"

"And . . . other things," she said hesitantly.

Calvin stepped closer. Clumsily, he took her in his arms. Her eyes closed . . . and then opened. He leaned over and kissed her.

"I shall never forget this moment," Katey whispered as they moved apart. Then she turned and hurried into the castle.

It was over all too fast. "Hey!" Calvin called. "Where are you going?"

"To sleep. And dream. Of you." She vanished down the corridor like a beautiful vision.

Calvin slumped against the wall. He cocked his head at a stone gargoyle. "You're lucky," he confided. "You're made of stone."

He stared at the gargoyle for another moment. Suddenly he ran into the castle as fast as he could.

"I'll walk you to your room," he said breathlessly as he caught up with Katey.

She half smiled and looked at him questioningly.

He took her hand. "Old Reseda custom."

"The more I hear of Reseda, the more I want to see it."

"I wish I could take you there." Calvin missed his family a lot now, but he knew he would miss Katey just as much when he got home. If he ever did.

"Good night," Katey said at the door to her room.

He walked slowly back to his room, then, on an impulse, hurried back again down the corridor to her room.

"Sssst! Princess?" he whispered to the door, after knocking once. "I haven't had so much fun in my whole life. I know you're worried about your father. Me, too. I promise I'll do everything I can to keep Lord Belasco from messing things up." He paused. "I guess that's it." He waited a moment, but he didn't hear anything.

"Oh, yeah. You're a great kisser." He hurried away, wishing only that he could have seen her face as he delivered his message.

IX
KIDNAPPED!

 Inside the room, Katey was not smiling at Calvin's message. It was hard to feel romantic with Ratan holding a hand over her mouth and a knife to her throat. As if that weren't bad enough, he smelled like he hadn't taken a bath in months.

"Wise girl," he grunted. "Any noise, and it would have been your last." He dragged her across the room to the wall, where he felt along the runes until he found the right one. The wall clicked open, and he dragged Katey into the secret passage.

*　　*　　*

Meanwhile, Lord Belasco stood waiting in the deserted Great Hall. "Thank you for meeting me at such short notice, Princess." He addressed the shadows.

Clad in a nightgown, Sarah stepped out. "Your servant said I would be supremely interested in what you had to say," she said coolly.

"He did not exaggerate," Lord Belasco said.

"Then say it and I shall be on my way." She moved impatiently toward the door. Lord Belasco grabbed her by the neck and hauled her back.

"How *dare* you!" she cried furiously, flailing her arms. "When my father hears how you have treated me, he'll—"

Lord Belasco thrust his face in front of hers. "I did not bring you here to listen to any more of your incessant royal prattle. Keep your mouth shut—and your sister will remain in good health," he hissed.

He released her, and Sarah drew back, horrified. "My sister? What have you done to my sister?"

"She is safe," Lord Belasco said. "For now. But I am tired of waiting for you to accept my offer."

"You're mad. You cannot force me to marry you."

"If you do not consent," he said slowly and distinctly, "the Princess Katherine will die."

Once more, he pulled her close. "This pact is

between you and me. If you say one word of this to anyone, you will never see your sister again. I await your answer. You have until the tournament."

*   *   *

Calvin lay on his bed, thinking of Katey. This was the most wonderful day of his life, he thought. There was no other girl like her.

Suddenly the door burst open. "You are under arrest for the murder of the Princess Katherine," Lord Belasco announced crisply. He nodded to his guards. "Take him."

As the guards sprang toward him, Calvin jumped aside and they tumbled together in a pile on his bed. Calvin leaped onto the floor, snatched up his backpack, and swung it at Lord Belasco's face. The evil lord toppled backward, and Calvin raced into the corridor with the guards hard on his heels.

"Get that boy!" He heard Lord Belasco shriek. "Kill him!"

In his nightshirt, Calvin ran faster down the corridor than he'd ever run in his life. His mind was a jumble of thoughts. Katey dead? How could it be? And they thought he had murdered her! He moaned. Then someone reached out from the shadows and yanked him into an alcove. A hand covered his mouth.

"Calvin!" Sarah whispered in an urgent voice. "I must speak to you of Katey!"

"I didn't do it!" he whispered back in a panic. "All we did was go on a picnic! Nothing weird happened. I swear I didn't kill her!"

"I know you did not kill her," Sarah soothed him.

"You do? How?"

"Because she is not dead."

He gave a huge sigh of relief and happiness. Katey was alive!

"She has been kidnapped under Lord Belasco's orders," Sarah continued. "I need your help."

"You do?"

"You must bring her back!"

He opened his mouth to reply, but Sarah laid a restraining hand on his lips as a squad of guards rushed past.

"They're looking for me," Calvin whispered. "Lord Belasco tried to arrest me."

"Then you have only one chance. . . ."

"Just one, huh?" Calvin asked nervously.

"My father."

Calvin shook his head. What did he have to do? He would do anything to save Katey, but how was he to get King Arthur to believe him? Lord Belasco had the King firmly under his thumb.

"Give him this." Sarah handed a white embroidered hankerchief to Calvin. "He will know you speak the truth."

Calvin gazed at the hanky. He hoped it would work. It seemed too easy to be true. With a sigh, he stuffed it into his pocket. Sarah motioned to Calvin to stay where he was, then she stepped out of the alcove. "Guards!" she called in an imperious voice.

The guards rushed to her side. "He went this way!" she told them, pointing.

"This way, men!" cried the head guard. As they all rushed off, Calvin crept out and headed in the opposite direction.

*   *   *

The door to King Arthur's bedchamber burst open. Arthur was startled awake and reached for the royal crown on the pillow beside him.

"Aha! By Merlin's prophecies!" he cried. "You come to take me in my sleep! Well, you won't take me *that* easily!"

He snatched a sword and brandished it in front of him. "Come into the light, you cowards!"

Calvin stepped forward.

"Calvin!" The King saluted him eagerly. "Just in time! Which way did they flee? How many were there? Five? Ten? Ahhh, the royal blood is pumping now! I have not felt this alive in years! My God! I feel strong! Leave us ride after the interlopers!"

King Arthur leaped to the floor and started to hurry past Calvin. "Sire, stop!" Calvin said, looking around the empty room. "There *are* no interlopers . . . or outerlopers!"

"Don't be ridiculous, boy!" Arthur scoffed. "Get my wardrobe ready! We're on the hunt!"

Calvin grabbed the King's sleeve. He had to make him listen. "Katey has been kidnapped!"

"Kidnapped? My baby is sleeping with the goats?"

"She's been taken away!"

"That's impossible!" Arthur cried out.

"Orders from Lord Belasco."

"Lord Belasco?" Arthur stopped, a stunned expression on his face. "But I trust Lord Belasco with my life. . . ."

"That is a very bad idea, Sire," Calvin told him. "You've been faked out. Played for a sucker. You got it stuck to you big-time. Your chain has been royally pulled."

"All right, boy," Arthur said wearily. "I get the point."

"Lord Belasco plans on stealing Camelot from

you," Calvin continued. "Just like he stole Katey."

Arthur shook his head. "No, I cannot believe it."

Calvin pulled the hankerchief from the pocket of his nightshirt. It seemed so flimsy. Why hadn't Sarah given him a better token of trust for the King? He could only hope this would get the message across.

The King was silent for a long moment as he gazed at the hankerchief. "No one knows of this signal but my daughters," he said at last in a hushed voice. "So . . . it is all true. . . ."

A loud knock sounded at the door, startling them both. Arthur motioned to Calvin to hide himself. Then he went to the door and flung it open.

Lord Belasco stood before him, cool and composed.

"Why are you disturbing my sleep, Lord Belasco?" Arthur demanded in a rage.

"My King," Lord Belasco began in mournful tones. "I have some terrible news. The Princess Katherine. She is dead."

"Dead? My Katey?! My poor Katey. Ohhhh!" Arthur cried in fake grief. "Who could have done this?"

"Calvin of Reseda," Lord Belasco purred.

"Calvin of Reseda!" the King roared. "After I fed him and clothed him, this is how he thanks me?

Why are you wasting my time? Find that boy! Bring me his head on a pike!"

Lord Belasco smiled with satisfaction. "Consider it done. . . ."

*   *   *

Arthur stared at his suit of armor. "I'm doomed," he said, comparing his waistline to the size of the armor. "Yon armor has remained in check these many years, while I have widened me territories."

"You can go on a diet *after* we save Camelot," Calvin said.

Arthur frowned. "Diet?"

"No boar's snouts."

"No more boar's snouts?" Arthur cried.

Calvin looked around the room. "Anyway, we're gonna have to go in disguise."

"Disguise?"

"Yeah. I figure if we look like miserable, starving, pathetic peasants, no one will notice."

"Peasants!" Arthur said, almost laughing. "Don't be ridiculous, boy. The royal wardrobe is designed to strike fear in the hearts of my enemies."

"Not anymore it doesn't."

The King locked eyes with Calvin. "What do you know, boy?"

Calvin stared at the King, trying to gauge how

much he should tell him. Should he tell him the whole truth? Did the King really want to know? Did he care?

"They hate you," he finally said.

"Hate me . . ." The King's face paled.

"Lord Belasco has been stealing from your people for years. There is nothing but starvation and sickness in Camelot. They think you don't care about them."

"Hate me . . ." Arthur repeated in a daze.

"You *do care*, don't you?"

The King looked up. "Of course I do, lad." Arthur pulled himself together. "Come. I know a way out."

* * *

Ratan dragged Katey into a cell and threw her in, then slammed the door shut.

"What are you going to do with me?" Katey asked, trying to keep her voice from trembling.

"Nothing," Ratan said. "If your sister gives herself to Lord Belasco in betrothal . . ."

"And if she doesn't?"

Ratan grinned widely. Then he ran a gloved forefinger straight across his throat.

X

OUT AND ABOUT

 "I rather like this," Arthur said, tipping his hood at a passing lady. "Out among my people. Getting my ears wet."

He and Calvin, disguised as peasants, were making their way through town. The King patted a little boy on the head and smiled fondly at him.

Suddenly a stream of water cascaded down, drenching Arthur's head and shoulders. A washerwoman had emptied her basin out the window, right on his head.

"Watch whom you bathe, washerwoman!" he roared.

"Washerwoman, eh?" she yelled back. "And who might you be then? The bloody King of England?" She laughed uproariously while the people on the street joined in.

Arthur drew himself up. "As a matter of fact, *I am* your King."

That provoked even more laughter.

"Oh, very nice," retorted the washerwoman. "And I am Cleobleedingpatra."

"By the sword Excalibur," Arthur said. "If thou were a man, I'd call you out!"

The washerwoman had a ready answer. "If *you* were a man, I'd throw more than a *bath* on you!"

A dead fish aimed with great accuracy hit King Arthur on the head. Calvin grabbed his arm and hauled him away from the still-laughing crowd.

"Look, Your Highness," he said, when they had escaped to a quieter street. "I don't want to insult you or anything, but are you nuts? This isn't the castle where everyone kisses your feet because they don't want to get cut out of the will—this is the real, in-your-face, carjacking, drive-by-shooting, kill-you-for-your-Reeboks street life!"

Arthur stared at him blankly. "What language do you speak, boy?"

"Let me give it to you straight," Calvin said.

"They find out you're the King—you're dead meat."

"First I am hit with a fish," Arthur said bemusedly. "Now you speak of dead meat." He looked around him. "All this talk of food makes me hungry. Let's eat."

"Your Lordship? What about Katey?"

"Well, she can join us!" Arthur said reasonably.

Calvin felt like shaking him. Sometimes he really liked this king, and other times . . . "She's been kidnapped!" he said.

"Right!" Arthur agreed, finally understanding. "There's no time for supper!"

Two guards appeared behind them. Calvin tugged on Arthur's sleeve, trying to get his attention, but the King ignored him.

"We must rescue my daughter," Arthur continued in a loud voice. "Your King has spoken!"

"He has, has he?" snarled one of the guards, marching up to Arthur and laying a heavy hand on his shoulder. "Arrest him!" the guard ordered.

"Hey!" Calvin cried. He tried to push the guard aside, but the guard yanked Calvin's hood off and drew his sword.

"Ah . . . the murderer!" he said.

Calvin whacked him with his staff, then whipped around just in time to block the second guard's move.

He looked past the second guard for a moment, and called out, "Don't do it, Sire!"

As the second guard automatically turned to see what was happening, Calvin smashed his staff into the back of the guard's knees. Then he smacked the staff into his stomach, tumbling him backward into a trough of pig slop.

"Lesson one," Calvin repeated with satisfaction. "Never take your eyes off your opponent."

The first guard sneaked up behind Calvin, but Arthur grabbed a bag of fertilizer and smashed it down on his head. "Oh, no you don't!" the King cried.

The guard stumbled in a daze toward the pig slop and toppled in just as the other guard was getting out. With a splat and a burble, they both sank deep into the muck.

* * *

Arthur and Calvin pressed themselves against a wall to avoid being seen by roving guards. "We are lost!" Arthur cried in despair. "We shall never reach the Princess in time!"

Calvin thought for a minute. "Yes, we will!"

A few minutes later, Calvin was pedaling furiously down the road on his blacksmith-forged mountain bike. His staff and the King's staff were both lashed to the frame. This time not Katey but Arthur was perched on the handlebars.

"This is sorcery! We're going to dieeeee! ..." Arthur yelled.

The bike sped down a hill, wobbling madly. Calvin lost control and he and the King both went hurtling off the bike and into the brush at the side of the road.

Calvin got to his feet and dusted himself off. "Are you okay, Your Highness?"

"If okay means a sore bottom, then yes," the King said wryly.

Somewhere nearby, a horse whinnied. They turned to look and saw two horses grazing in a field. None other than the Black Knight was watching over them on his mighty steed.

"After him!" Arthur cried, ready to charge the Black Knight even without his own horse.

"Chill out!" Calvin said. "He's on *our* side."

With a nod, the Black Knight galloped away, leaving behind the two horses in the field for Calvin and Arthur.

"I do not understand," Arthur said in bewilderment.

"Let's go." Calvin gestured toward the horses. There would be time to explain later.

They swung onto their mounts and galloped off to save Katey.

XI

RESCUE

 Under cover of dense forest, Arthur and Calvin waited for a squad of Lord Belasco's soldiers to pass by. Then they rode off in the opposite direction.

"Lord Belasco's men are everywhere," Calvin commented. He looked over at the King, who wore a distant expression on his face.

"What's the matter?" Calvin asked.

"I cannot believe what a blind fool I've been. How can I be a king when I know nothing of my kingdom?" the King burst out.

He had been doing some serious thinking during their ride through the forest. "The Black Knight, whom I believed to be my enemy, is the true deliverer of my people, and my most trusted confidant . . . is a traitor."

They stopped for a moment to let the horses rest.

"I am deeply troubled, lad," Arthur went on. "When I was a boy, much the same as you, I could not face the things I feared. It was by sheer accident that I pulled the sword Excalibur from the stone. Oh, it's true, over the years I did indeed grow into a strong king."

He held the reins loosely and stared down at his gnarled hands. "But now, alas, I feel I've become that cowering boy again. I've lost all belief in myself. If *I* cannot believe in myself, who will?"

Calvin realized that Arthur felt the way *he* had, back in Reseda. He tried to remember what *his* father had said to him when he felt that way. "Where *I* come from, Sire, there *are* no swords in stones that turn dweebs like me into heroes. I used to think I needed one. But you know what? I don't."

Arthur smiled at him. "You're a good man, Calvin Fuller. Come. The sun is setting. We must go on. I won't let my people down."

*   *   *

Arthur and Calvin waded through the moat together, toward Merlin's castle. The water was frigid. Calvin thought how glad he'd be when they got out of it. Arthur was covered in grass and water lilies. What a sight he looked! Calvin looked equally ridiculous.

"This is totally impossible!" Calvin protested. The castle was dark and forbidding. "There's no way into this place!"

"How did you say it?" the King retorted. *"Chill out?"*

They climbed out of the cold, dark water. Holding up his hand to guide Calvin, Arthur led the way around the castle to a secret passage.

"Cool!" Calvin cried.

Arthur nodded proudly. "Merlin showed it to me long ago when I played here as a boy."

Quietly, they entered Merlin's castle and, carrying their staffs, tiptoed across the great main hall. The sound of faint crying came from somewhere below in the castle. Calvin caught his breath. It was Katey!

"He has her in the dungeon!" Arthur whispered. He sounded fierce and furious. He sounded like the King Arthur of old.

They walked silently down a cold stone corridor

with ancient jail cells cut into its sides. A guard stood at a stairway entrance. Silently, using only gestures, Arthur and Calvin planned out their attack.

Arthur walked boldly up to the guard and planted himself in front of the man. "Have you not learned to bow in the presence of the King, you dog?" he roared.

As the guard stared at him in shock, Calvin crept around behind him and brought his staff down firmly on his head. The guard crumpled without a sound.

They hurried down the stone stairs. Katey was huddled in the corner of a cell, her eyes wide with fear, watching a large rat with hungry red eyes make its way toward her.

"Katey!" Calvin cried. Thank goodness she was all right!

She leaped up and rushed to the bars. "I knew you'd come!"

Calvin rattled the door. "You wouldn't happen to have a key, would you?" he asked Arthur.

"I have something far better," Arthur said proudly. "A father's love for his daughter—and a king's shoulder."

He moved away, then boldly charged the door.

"Ooof!" The King had landed on the floor. "I am

sorry, lad, I am no match for Merlin's door."

"Maybe not . . ." Calvin pulled his Swiss Army knife from his backpack with a flourish. "But *this* is!"

Rapidly he set to work picking the lock.

"What sorcery is this?" Arthur asked with amazement.

Calvin jiggled the tool to the left, then to the right. There! He almost had it. "Swiss Army knife," he said absently.

"Swiss Army knife," Katey breathed. "The very *name* conjures up greatness."

"Yeah, it's right up there with Harley-Davidson," Calvin agreed.

As the King and his daughter exchanged puzzled looks, the lock clicked, and the door swung open.

XII
RATAN'S END

 Calvin, Katey, and the King tiptoed down the corridor, ran up the stairs, and began to cross the main hall.

"Your Majesty. How nice of you to drop by," Ratan snarled from the balcony. A few minutes earlier, he had found a Mad Dog Bubble Gum wrapper on the floor of the main hall. He had recognized it instantly. Now he was ready for them. They would not escape this time!

"Seize them!" he cried in his hoarse voice.

Guards rushed out from all directions.

"We're in big trouble," Calvin said.

The King cried out, "What I wouldn't give for Excalibur!"

Calvin unwrapped his staff and pulled out the shining sword concealed within. "You've got it!"

"I have?" Arthur cried out in surprise. "Oh! It has been too long!"

As the guards charged them, Calvin held out the sword to the king. "Just do it!"

Arthur nodded, took the sword, and hefted it. A bright light blazed out. Strength, energy, and youth seemed to flow from the sword directly into him.

The three of them began to fight off the attacking guards.

"Jammin'!" Calvin yelled gleefully.

Arthur paused and looked at him quizzically. "Jammin'?" Without waiting for an answer, the King raised Excalibur high and dispatched two guards with a single swift stroke. He looked thirty years younger.

Calvin dove out of the way of two broadswords. As he rolled over and rose to his feet, two more guards attacked him. In the split second before he whipped out his nunchaku, he noticed the great chandelier hanging from the ceiling. Whirling the nunchaku, he whacked one guard on the chin and the other on the back of the head.

Now, if only he could cut the rope holding the chandelier! As if she had read his mind, from the other side of the room Katey tossed him a sword. He leaped and cut the rope. Nothing happened. "Gee, this *always* works in the movies," he muttered.

Meanwhile, Arthur was busily swinging Excalibur around, striking one guard, then another, knocking them out cold.

Suddenly Ratan crept up behind Katey, grabbed her, and swiftly dragged her up the stone steps.

Katey screamed loudly.

"Katherine!" shouted the King. As Calvin swung around, Arthur pointed. "He's up there!"

The two of them dashed up the stairs in pursuit.

*   *   *

It was dark on the rampart as Ratan pulled a kicking and screaming Katey up higher and higher.

"Ratan!" Arthur called. "That's far enough! Let my daughter go!"

In response, Ratan shoved a knife under Katey's chin and forced her to the very edge of a precipice.

Panting, Arthur and Calvin flung themselves up onto the rampart.

"Stop or she flies like a bird!" Ratan snarled.

Arthur and Calvin halted. They were only a few

feet away from Ratan—and Katey. Calvin cautiously stepped forward. "Let her go," he said. "Take me."

Ratan jabbed the knife blade closer to Katey's throat. "Stay put or her blood will be on your hands, boy!"

Arthur leaned close to Calvin and whispered, "If we both charge at once, maybe one of us will get to her in time."

"Wait," Calvin whispered back. "I have a better idea." He pulled his portable CD player from his tunic and began to fiddle with it.

"I'm afraid rock and roll will not work this time," Ratan sneered.

"You're wrong. It is the great . . . equalizer," Calvin said with a little smile.

In answer, Ratan pushed Katey closer to the edge.

Suddenly a ruby red laser beam shot out of the CD player, straight into Ratan's eyes. Ratan cried out. His hands flew to his blinded eyes, and Katey ran to her father and Calvin.

Blinking to see, Ratan pulled his sword out and stepped toward Arthur.

"You are no match for Excalibur!" the King cried.

"You pathetic old man!" Ratan said hoarsely.

He lunged for the King. Arthur sidestepped neatly, then swung his sword with precision. Ratan jumped back to avoid it, and fell backward off the rampart. There was a scream, then a loud splash. Then all was silent. Ratan was gone.

"Oh, Calvin!" Katey cried. "I *knew* you'd come. I was so worried you were going to get hurt!"

Her father pretended that his feelings were wounded. "Hey. What am I? Pig vomit?"

"You're bad, Art," Calvin said approvingly. "Real bad."

*   *   *

They rode home in the dawn light.

"Poor Sarah," Katey said. Now that *her* troubles were over, she could worry about her sister. "She will never be happy if she is forced to marry the one she *does not* love."

She scowled at her father to make sure he got the point.

"What do you mean, Daughter?" Arthur asked. "She will marry the tournament champion. I could not have chosen a better husband for her *myself*."

"Exactly. *You* could not have chosen. What about Sarah? Should she not choose her own destiny?"

Arthur snorted. "Sarah choose her own husband? I've never *heard* of such a thing!"

"You never heard of the Round Table, either," Calvin pointed out.

Arthur was silent a moment. "Very well. I am willing to speak of this along the way."

"Thank you, Father," Katey said gratefully.

Arthur gazed at the rolling hills, the green grass, the tall, slender trees. Then he dismounted and motioned for Calvin and Katey to do the same. "This is as good a place as any," he said.

"Place for what, Sire?" Calvin asked, mystified.

"Kneel, lad," the King commanded in a solemn voice.

"Kneel?"

"Just do it," Katey whispered, her eyes brightening.

As Calvin knelt on the grass, Arthur stood before him with his great sword Excalibur upraised. "Calvin Fuller of Reseda. Do you swear allegiance to your King and kingdom?"

Calvin nodded, his eyes wide with wonder and delight.

"Do you swear to uphold the laws of Camelot? To always take the path of righteousness and goodness?"

"I'll try, Your Highness."

Arthur scowled at him.

"Okay, I will," Calvin said quickly.

"Then let all who witness this know," Arthur

continued, "it does not take a sword in the stone . . . to make a hero."

His eyes shone brightly as he kissed the blade of Excalibur and then formally brought it down flat on Calvin's shoulders. "By the sword Excalibur, I dub thee Knight of the Round Table."

It seemed to Calvin as he was kneeling that everything was giving off a strange and wonderful light—the trees, the grass, Katey's face. He, Calvin Fuller, was a Knight of the Round Table!

"Rise, *Sir* Calvin of Reseda," Arthur ordered.

As they went to their horses, King Arthur said to Calvin, "And now, Sir Knight, we have some unfinished business."

The king, his daughter, and a brand-new knight rode off toward Camelot.

XIII
THE TOURNAMENT

 In the Great Hall on Tournament Day, Sarah stood waiting. She had just told Kane she could not marry him. Lord Belasco crossed the threshold, went over to her, and bowed. "Thank you for coming," she said tonelessly.

"Your wish is my command, Princess," Lord Belasco said smoothly. "You have made your decision?"

"Yes." Sarah took a deep breath. This was the worst decision she had ever had to make. But her sister's life was more important than even her own happiness. "I will consent to marry you."

Lord Belasco smiled triumphantly. He moved closer to take her hand. "You were always the smart one in your family."

The door opened and light flooded the darkened room. Arthur, flanked by Katey and Calvin, marched in triumphantly.

Sarah rushed to her sister and held her tight in her arms. Then, glancing at her father and the sword Excalibur, she said, "I see you have your old friend with you, Father."

"Indeed I do, Daughter. I, too, am delivered." He glared fiercely at Lord Belasco.

"You look well, Your Majesty," Lord Belasco stuttered. He was unnerved. This was not the meek, cringing Arthur he had once ordered around, manipulated, and despised. "Now if you will excuse me—I must prepare for the tournament."

As Lord Belasco walked quickly from the room, Calvin turned to the King. "You gotta be kidding. You're going to let him walk, after all he's done? Well, *I'm* not." He started running after Lord Belasco, but Arthur thrust Excalibur in front of him.

"Remember," the King said, "the people believe

me to be a coward. And the guards are still loyal to Lord Belasco. Bide your time, young knight. When the hour is right . . . we'll nail him."

*   *   *

It was a happy, festive crowd at the tournament. Ladies in colorful gowns cheered knights mounted on shining steeds. Musicians sang. Vendors hawked sweets. Children ran in and out among the stands.

In the King's box, Arthur stood up, holding Excalibur above his head. The crowd became silent.

"My people! My people!" the King called out.

A low muttering went through the crowd. They were not fond of him, he could see that now. Still, he would say what he had to say.

"You come from the land. As do I. I was but a stable boy when I pulled Excalibur from the stone. And you made me your King. Together, over the years, we made Camelot great. And then . . ." Arthur took a deep breath. Now was the time for truth, painful as it was. "I turned my back on you. I betrayed your trust."

The crowd murmured approvingly.

"My people," the King announced, taking strength from their approval, "I shall fail you no more!"

This time they cheered him.

"From this day forth, the tournament shall be open to *all* free men," Arthur proclaimed. "Let it be known that the great sword Excalibur, Camelot, *and* my daughter's hand shall go to my successor—the last man unhorsed in this honorable combat."

The crowd cheered wildly. "Let the tournament begin!" Arthur cried.

Lord Belasco clenched his jaw. He turned toward the King's box and locked eyes with Master Kane. Impertinent fool! He'd wipe that awestuck, overjoyed look off his face. No low-born weapons master was going to steal Sarah from him! He, Lord Belasco, would win this tournament, whatever it took.

*   *   *

Calvin helped his teacher, Kane, into an armored breastplate. Then he reached into his pocket and pulled out a candy bar. "Here. I have been saving this for an emergency."

Kane wrinkled his nose. "Is it food?"

"Compared to what you're used to," Calvin muttered under his breath, "it's gourmet dining."

Kane took the candy in his armored gloves and clumsily brought it to his mouth. "Mmmmm!" His face lit up. "You are truly a great knight!"

"Sir Kane," a squire interrupted. "'Tis time, sir."

Master Kane rode into position, licked one last bit of chocolate from his hand, and lowered his visor.

It took him only a moment to unseat his first opponent. The crowd cheered wildly, but Sarah, leaping to her feet, cheered the loudest.

"Yessssssss!" yelled Calvin.

One by one, Kane vanquished his opponents with his expert lance. One other knight also won victory after victory. Finally, only the two of them were left on the field: Lord Belasco and Master Kane.

As they rode up to the King's box, Arthur addressed them: "You have defeated all opponents. Only one of you shall leave the field of honor and one day rule in my stead."

Lord Belasco looked haughtily at Kane, then galloped off. Arthur leaned over his box and murmured to Kane, "Kick his butt."

As Kane lowered his visor and aimed his lance, Lord Belasco turned his glove over and revealed a shiny square of metal that reflected the sun with dazzling brightness.

Then they charged. They charged with more ferocity and power than any two previous opponents. As Kane came closer, Lord Belasco again turned his glove over and aimed the reflective square straight at Kane's eyes, momentarily blinding

Kane. Then he rammed into him and Kane tumbled sideways.

But Kane hung on! Snatching at the horse's mane, slumped over, he stayed on, though he could not fight anymore.

A distraught Sarah fled from the King's box.

"I fear Kane is defeated!" Arthur cried sadly.

"Hey! You know the rules!" Calvin reminded him. "He's still on his horse!"

"He is right, Father!" Katey said. "As long as he is on his steed, he is still in the game!"

"Stall him!" Calvin had an idea. It just might work. "I'll be right back!"

Lord Belasco approached the King's box. "It is done," he said in tones of deep satisfaction. "Pronounce my victory."

"Lord Belasco," Arthur said sternly, "as you have not unhorsed Master Kane, he is not defeated."

"But, Sire!" Lord Belasco protested.

"Rules are rules," Arthur told him.

Lord Belasco scowled at him. Interfering old man! "Very well, I shall await the alloted time. Then you must proclaim my victory."

"I can hardly wait," said Arthur as Lord Belasco rode off.

"Hurry, Calvin," Katey urged. She closed her eyes

tightly. For Sarah's sake, as well as for the sake of Camelot, he had to help Master Kane!

*   *   *

Behind the tent, Calvin was helping a dazed, barely conscious Kane off his horse. "Master Kane! Master Kane!" He slapped his face lightly. "How many fingers am I holding up?"

"Just a little off the top," Kane slurred, his eyes rolling. "Keep the sideburns."

"He speaks in tongues!" cried his frightened squire. He started to run in the direction of the King's box. Calvin grabbed his arm. "Where are you going?"

"To announce his defeat."

"He isn't defeated!" Calvin insisted. "He's . . . meditating!"

The squire squatted and picked up Kane's limp wrist. It fell heavily to the ground.

"I fear he is dead, sir," said the squire.

"Listen!" Calvin said fiercely. He wasn't going to give up that easily. "Who's the squire and who's the knight?"

*   *   *

At the King's box, Lord Belasco was waiting impatiently. "The time has passed, Your Majesty. Kane is defeated."

Katey jumped triumphantly to her feet. "Wrong again—dweeb!" She pointed across the field.

As Kane reentered the ring astride his steed, the crowd cheered enthusiastically. Arthur breathed a deep sigh of relief. Katey jumped up and down with excitement. With a sneer, Lord Belasco spurred his horse back into position.

Kane lumbered out to joust position, his armor somehow much looser, clanking and bouncing as he rode.

His squire covered his eyes with his hands.

Lord Belasco smiled cynically, then lowered his visor, picked up his lance, and charged.

Kane too lowered his lance. It wobbled slightly. He steadied it and charged.

As the two horsemen passed, Lord Belasco threw his lance at Kane, and neatly sliced off his head.

The crowd gasped. Arthur stared in horror. Katey flung herself into her father's arms.

But the now-headless Kane did not fall. He galloped to the end of the lane and readied his lance for attack once more.

"'Tis black magic!" Lord Belasco muttered. He was stunned, for once, into immobility.

The headless Kane charged with wild determination, planting his lance in Lord Belasco's chest and toppling him off his horse. As Kane raised his lance in victory, Lord Belasco sat on the ground, disheveled and furious.

A head emerged from the gaping hole in the armor. It was Calvin! "You're history, Lord Belasco."

"Your blood is mine!" Lord Belasco jumped to his feet and rushed at Calvin with insane fury.

"Hey! Chill out!" Calvin yelled. This guy wasn't fooling.

Lord Belasco yanked Calvin off his horse and unsheathed his sword. "Prepare to meet thy ancestors," he snarled.

As he raised his sword to behead Calvin, a black arrow thunked into his gauntlet. His sword dropped to the ground. He turned and gaped. The Black Knight was there, sitting high and proud on his horse, charging toward him!

His face set grimly, Lord Belasco kicked Calvin out of the way. Then he stomped over to a knight on horseback, snatched his shield and a ball and mace, and turned to face the Black Knight.

Lord Belasco blocked the first blow with his borrowed shield. He swung his mace ferociously. The Black Knight shielded himself just in time. He jumped off his horse and advanced toward the evil lord.

The Black Knight slapped Lord Belasco on the head with the blade of his sword, then slammed it into his side. He elbowed Lord Belasco in the face, kicked him in the rear, spanked him with his sword, and finally pinned him against a wall, with his sword at his throat.

Breathless and astounded, Lord Belasco stared at him. He had never lost a match before, except by trickery! The Black Knight pushed the blade closer to his throat. Finally Lord Belasco dropped his sword. He was beaten.

XIV
THE WINNER

 The Black Knight and Calvin marched triumphantly toward the King's box.

"You won the tournament, Sir Calvin!" Arthur said. "Sarah's hand is yours."

"Sarah!" Calvin cried, aghast. "But I hardly know her."

"It is not a question of familiarity, it is a question of victory." As Katey glared at him, Arthur added almost plaintively, "Isn't it?"

"No, Father. It is not," Katey said firmly.

"It doesn't matter, Your Highness," Calvin hastened to say. "I'm not the champion." He pointed to the Black Knight. "He is."

Arthur nodded. "It seems I owe you more than one debt of gratitude, Sir Knight. Reveal thyself, so that we all may know thee."

The Black Knight bowed and then began to work the helmet latches.

All the people around quieted. Who *was* the Black Knight, who had been their benefactor and protector? No one had ever known, though many had speculated.

Finally, the helmet was undone. The Black Knight pulled it off, and long brown hair cascaded over the black armor. "Hello, Father," said Sarah.

Arthur sat down in astonishment. His *daughter* was the Black Knight? Katey and Calvin applauded wildly, along with the crowds of people gathered around the King's box.

When Arthur regained his composure, he gazed first at Kane, then at Sarah. "You have won the right to choose, Daughter," he said, beaming at her.

"Thank you, Father." She and Kane embraced, as two guards dragged Lord Belasco forward.

Arthur's smile vanished. "And as for you, Lord Belasco, thou art banished from this kingdom forever. If I were you, I wouldn't stop until you reach . . ."

97

"Cucamunga," Calvin supplied.

"Yes," Arthur agreed. "Cucamunga."

Lord Belasco glared one last time and then was led away.

* * *

Sarah and Kane came over to Calvin.

"Thank you," Sarah said, giving him a hug.

Kane stuck out his hand. "You are a fine knight."

"I had a great teacher," Calvin said.

Arthur added, "My kingdom is at your disposal. What do you want? A castle? A dukedom?"

Calvin sighed. He had come to know and love Camelot. But he still missed his family. More than ever! He hoped they weren't worried about him. "I just want to go home," he said.

* * *

In the King's sanctuary, Arthur and Katey watched as Calvin knelt before the Well of Destiny. Once more the water clouded and Merlin's face appeared.

"You have done well, brave knight," the magician said. "Arthur and Camelot are restored to glory. And now, as promised, I will show you the way home."

His face wrinkled and rippled, then disappeared. A vortex grew in the water until it filled the entire well.

"Godspeed, Sir Calvin," King Arthur said.

Calvin threw his arms around him. "You've given me so much," he said. "Is there anything I can give you?"

"No . . . well . . . yes . . ." Arthur looked embarrassed. "I wouldn't mind that Swiss Army knife."

Calvin pulled it out of his backpack and handed it to the King. Then he turned to Katey.

"Is there nothing I can say or do to make you stay?" she pleaded.

He sighed deeply and took her in his arms. "I have to go back," he said gently. "I mean forward."

"You won't forget me?"

"How could I?" Their eyes met and they embraced once more. Then with one parting look at his friends, Calvin jumped into the vortex and disappeared into the mists of time.

XV
HOME RUN

 Calvin's eyes popped open. Once again he was sitting on the end of the dugout bench. He turned to the boy next to him.

"I'm back!" he announced triumphantly. "There wasn't any earthquake!"

His teammate looked at him like he was crazy.

"You're up, Fuller!" shouted the coach.

Calvin stood and walked toward the plate.

"Ventilate him, Calvin!" yelled one of his teammates.

"Merlin brought me back before I struck out!" Calvin said to himself in surprise. "He gave me another chance!"

"Try swinging this time, Fuller," Howell, the perfect athlete, sneered.

"Thanks, Howell. Love your tan," Calvin retorted.

Howell stared at him in a puzzled way as Calvin moved past the stands.

"It's only a game, Son," his father called. "Just give it your best shot."

"Good luck, honey, we're all rooting for you," his mother said.

His sister Maya leaned against the fence. "If you get killed, I get your room!" she taunted.

Calvin leaned over and kissed her through the fence. "You want my room? You got it."

As he walked up to the bat rack, he stole a look at Ricky Baker. The pitcher was grinning maniacally and slapping the ball into his glove.

"You're dead meat, Fuller." Ricky took off his hat to wipe the sweat from his forehead, and Calvin saw, for the first time, a lightning streak of white running through his jet-black hair. Like Lord Belasco's, Calvin thought with a jolt.

The coach approached him. "Look, just remember what I told you. . . ."

This time, Calvin remembered. "Three things, right, Coach?"

The coach stared at him. Then he slapped Calvin on the shoulder. "Go for it, kid."

Calvin pulled Howell's big bat out of the rack and went over to the plate.

THUMP! The ball hit the catcher's mitt.

"Steeee-rike one!" yelled the umpire.

Ricky Baker sneered, but Calvin ignored him. He had just seen something written in ancient letters on the bat. The word *Excalibur.*

With renewed confidence, Calvin readied himself for the next pitch. "Not this time, Baker," he said to himself.

The smile left Ricky Baker's face. There was something different about Calvin today. He wasn't the cringing nerd Ricky had come to count on. He spit on the ball and wound up for a fast one.

Calvin swung. THUNK! He knocked the ball out of the park. A home run!

The crowd went wild, screaming and cheering. Calvin ran around the bases, behind the player who had been on second. The boy touched home plate and then pulled off his hat.

It was Katey! In a baseball uniform, of course. She waited for him with a huge smile on her face.

As Calvin crossed home plate, scoring the winning point, Katey slapped him a high five.

"Nice going, Fuller!" She looked like Katey—but she sounded like any American girl.

"Thanks," Calvin said. "Your name's Katey, right?"

"That's me."

The parents crowded around to congratulate the team. Calvin's jaw dropped. He had just spotted King Arthur—in American clothes—whittling a piece of wood with a Swiss Army knife.

"Nice going, you two," Arthur said in an American accent.

"Thanks, Daddy," said Katey. "This is Calvin Fuller."

"Nice to meet you, Calvin. Awesome hit."

"Thanks, Your Highness," Calvin stuttered. "I mean, sir."

Calvin's mom and dad and his sister, Maya, crowded around him, hugging him and slapping his back. But he could only stare at Katey. "Thou want to go for pizza?"

Katey grinned. "Jammin'."